Gregory and the Magic Line

'A wonderful tale ... This is a fresh, exciting,
multi-coloured experience of a book with fabulous
illustrations that will inspire all young children
to be creative and imaginative.'
Bookseller

'A gloriously inventive picture book'
Carousel

'Exploration and creativity are the key themes of
Gregory and the Magic Line ... the story nurtures
the reader's enthusiasm for using his or her imagination.'
Child Education

D1334912

To Mum and Dad

Thank you for giving me "roots and wings"

First published in 2002 by
Orion Children's Books
This edition published 2003 by Dolphin paperbacks
a division of the Orion Publishing Group Ltd
Orion House
5 Upper St Martin's Lane
London WC2H 9EA

Text and illustrations copyright © Dawn Piggot 2002

The right of Dawn Piggot to be identified as the author and illustrator of this work has been asserted.

Designed by Sarah Hodder

A catalogue record for this book is available from the British Library
Printed and bound in Italy
ISBN 1 84255 278 3

Gregory and the Magic Line

Dawn Piggot

Dolphin

Gregory had a red pencil case,

and in the pencil case
lived a pencil,

and in the pencil
lived a magic line,

and the line wanted to get out.

"Take me for a walk,"
said the line.

"Draw me straight, draw me thick and draw me thin."

So Gregory drew the line

STRAIGHT,

and **thick**,

and thin.

"I like this," said the line.
"I like to be out."

But the line wanted more. **"Can't you make me shapes?"** said the line.

So Gregory drew

a square,

a rectangle,

a circle,

an oval,

and a triangle.

"This is great," said the line.
"I like being shapes. I can be

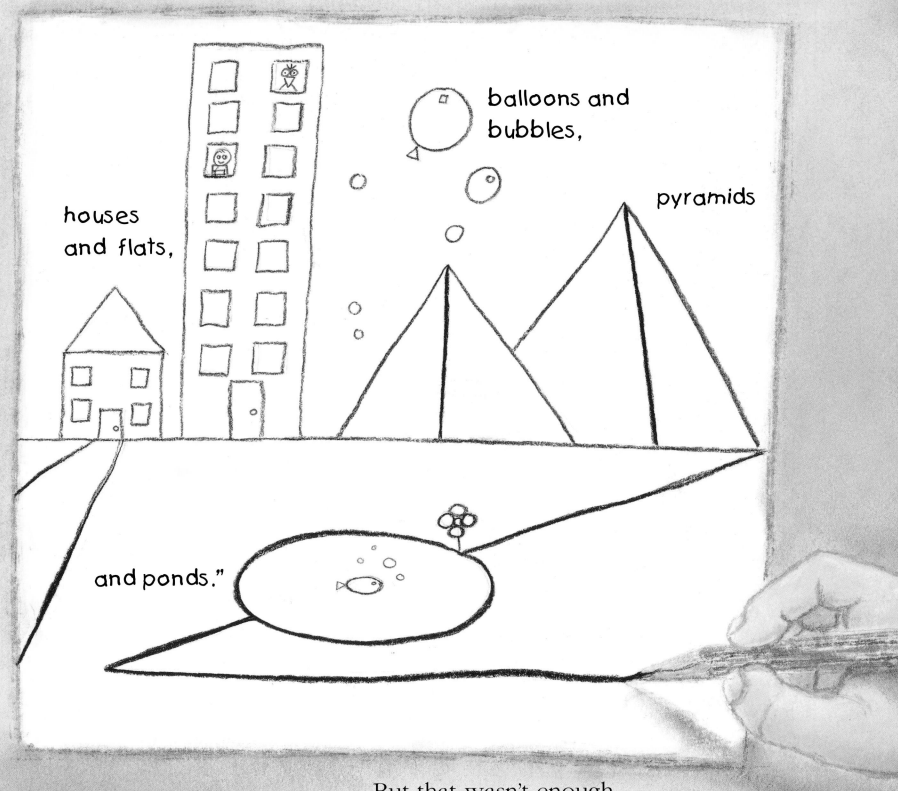

But that wasn't enough.

"I'm tired of just being black!" said the line.
"Make me change colour.
Make me yellow and red
and blue and green!"

So Gregory drew the line yellow and red
and blue and green...

"Now walk me faster," said the line.
"Make me **wiggly**,
with **curves**
and **dots**
and **dashes**."

So Gregory did.

"Look at me!" whooped the line.
"Now I can be coloured patterns,
and people with funny faces."

"Take me for a jog," said the line.
"Make me zigzags
and squiggles,
spots and slashes."

So Gregory made

zigzags

and *squiggles*

and spots

and *slashes*.

"I love this," said the line.
"Now I can be trees, grass and flowers,
lightning, rain and waves."

Gregory and the magic line were warming up.

"Take me for a run!" cried the line.
"Make me bold and detailed, dense and faint."
So Gregory drew a line that was

bold and
detailed,
dense
and faint.

"Wonderful!" said the line.
"Now I can be animals and birds!
I can be near and far away!"

Gregory made birds and animals. He made mice and elephants and ostriches and stripy tigers. He made snakes and frogs and spotty dogs.

He made them big and close up,

and small and *far away.*

"More! More!" shouted the line.

Gregory drew a sun and moon and stars.

He joined the stars up to make pictures in the sky. Then he drew cars and trains and boats on the sea.

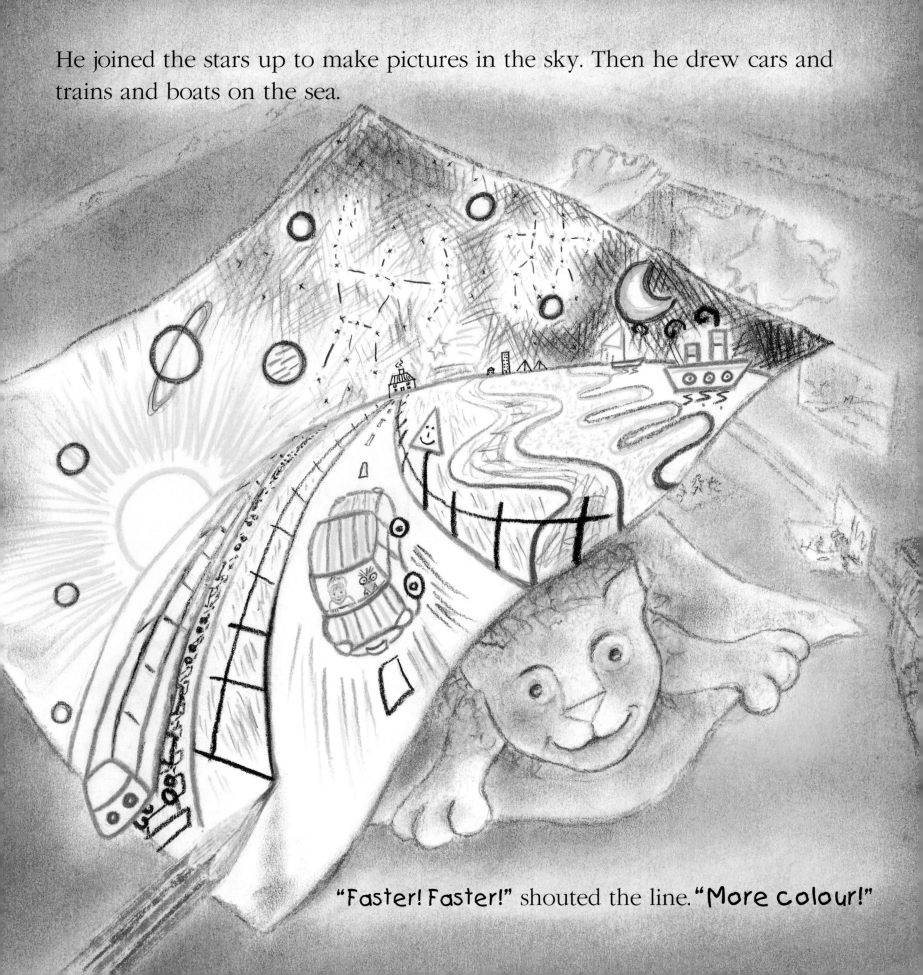

"Faster! Faster!" shouted the line. "More colour!"

So Gregory mixed yellow and blue and red and green together and made the line new colours. He made them bright, he made them pale, he made them dark. He mixed them *faster* and *faster*.

"Now put me all together and let's fly!" cried the line.

So Gregory *joined up* all the lines and they flew together.

High over Gregory's
land of lines
they swooped
and soared,
ducked and dived.

At last the line said, "I'm tired."
"I'm tired too," said Gregory.
"Let's go home."

So the line took Gregory home.

And he put the magic line back in his pencil and put the pencil into his red pencil case.

"**Goodnight,**" said the line.
"Goodnight," said Gregory.

"**Thanks for the walk,**" said the line.
"That's okay," said Gregory.